# Jon Scieszka's TRUCKTOWN

## SNOW TRUCKING!

### WRITTEN BY JON SCIESZKA

CHARACTERS AND ENVIRONMENTS DEVELOPED BY THE

DAVID SHANNON    LOREN LONG    DAVID GORDON

ILLUSTRATION CREW:

Executive producer: TOT INDUSTRIES in association with Animagic S.L.

Creative supervisor: Sergio Pablos ○ Drawings by: Juan Pablo Navas ○ Color by: Isabel Nadal

Color assistant: Gabriela Lazbal ○ Art director: Karin Paprocki

### READY-TO-ROLL

ALADDIN PAPERBACKS
NEW YORK    LONDON    TORONTO    SYDNEY

👑 ALADDIN PAPERBACKS

An imprint of Simon & Schuster Children's Publishing Division

1230 Avenue of the Americas, New York, NY 10020

Copyright © 2008 by JRS Worldwide, LLC

READY-TO-READ, ALADDIN PAPERBACKS, and related logo are

registered trademarks of Simon & Schuster, Inc.

TRUCKTOWN and JON SCIESZKA'S TRUCKTOWN and design are trademarks of JRS Worldwide, LLC.

The text of this book was set in Truck King.    Manufactured in the United States of America

10 9 8 7 6 5 4

Library of Congress Cataloging-in-Publication Data

Scieszka, Jon.    Snow trucking! / by Jon Scieszka ; artwork created by the Design Garage:

David Gordon, Loren Long, David Shannon.—1st Aladdin Paperbacks ed.

p. cm.—(Jon Scieszka's Trucktown. Ready-to-roll)

Summary: On a snow day, all the trucks go out to play.

ISBN-13: 978-1-4169-4140-8    ISBN-10: 1-4169-4140-1 (pbk)

ISBN-13: 978-1-4169-4151-4    ISBN-10: 1-4169-4151-7 (library)

[1. Trucks—Fiction. 2. Snow—Fiction] I. Design Garage. II. Gordon, David, 1965 Jan. 22- ill.

III. Long, Loren, ill. IV. Shannon, David, ill. V. Title.

PZ7.S41267Sn 2008    [E]—dc22    2007027152

Monday.
Snow.

Tuesday.

Snow.

Wednesday.

"Snow day?" asks Jack.

Ted's radio beeps.
Beep beep beep.

"Snow day!"
the radio beeps.
"Snow day!"
the trucks cheer.

"Ready? Set? GO day!" shouts Jack.

Gabby **skates.**
Kat **Slides.**

Jack shoots.
He SCORES!

# Then there is a CRAZY call.

"Do you want an ice cream?
Do you want an ice cream?
Do you want an ice cream?"

"Not on a snow day,
Izzy," says Jack.

# Melvin makes a snow truck.

Big Rig knocks it down.

Pete dumps.
Pete laughs.

Dan dumps.
Dan laughs last.

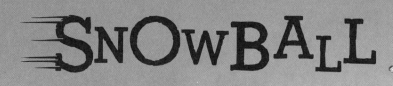

"Look at that!"
says Jack.

"We cleared ALL
the streets."

Now **THAT** is a
Trucktown Snow day.